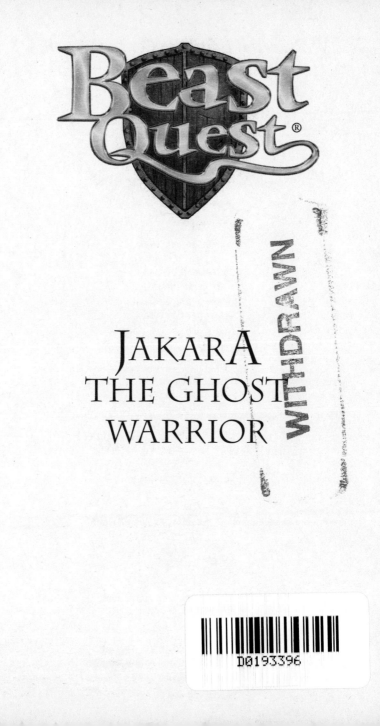

Beast Quest

JAKARA
THE GHOST
WARRIOR

With special thanks to Conrad Mason
To Madeleine St-Amour

www.beastquest.co.uk

ORCHARD BOOKS
Carmelite House
50 Victoria Embankment
London EC4Y 0DZ

A Paperback Original
First published in Great Britain in 2015

Beast Quest is a registered trademark of Beast Quest Limited
Series created by Beast Quest Limited, London

Text © Beast Quest Limited 2015
Cover and inside illustrations by Steve Sims © Beast Quest Limited
2015

A CIP catalogue record for this book is available from
the British Library.

ISBN 978 1 40833 497 3

3 5 7 9 10 8 6 4 2

Printed and bound by CPI Group (UK) Ltd, Croydon, CR0 4YY

Orchard Books
An imprint of Hachette Children's Group
Part of the Watts Publishing Group Limited
An Hachette UK Company

www.hachette.co.uk

JAKARA
THE GHOST
WARRIOR

BY ADAM BLADE

ORCHARD

STORY ONE

Aduro! Where are you, master?

I am so afraid... The wise Aduro has gone missing. I only hope he is still within the grounds of the Palace. No one knows better than my master what dangers lurk outside the city walls... And without his magic, he could come to terrible harm!

I have an idea where he might be, and it fills me with horror. The Chronicles of Avantia lie open on his desk – the last thing he was reading before his disappearance. I fear he has been dwelling once more on the death of his old master, Mivan, and on the fateful last Quest of Kara, Mistress of the Beasts.

If only he would leave that old tale alone! His curiosity could lead him down a dark and dangerous road, from which there is no return.

Daltec

Wizard of Avantia

CHAPTER ONE

DEADLY PERIL

"Give up," said Elenna. "You don't stand a chance!"

Tom sighed as he studied the painted board. Elenna's little wooden soldiers had his own trapped between a forest and a mountain, and she had just moved her catapults into range. *She's right*, he thought. He might have faced terrible dangers and vanquished countless Beasts, but when it came to the game of *Peril!*, he was as useless as a wizard without any magic.

On the other hand, Aduro doesn't have any magic, and he's far from useless!

Tom reached for a piece, moving his cavalry to attack Elenna's catapults.

"Are you sure about that?" asked Elenna, raising an eyebrow.

"Wait..." said Tom.

But it was too late. Elenna moved a carved wooden dragon out from the forest to attack Tom's cavalry from the right side.

"Your turn, Master of the Beasts," she said, with a wink.

Tom smiled. If only he could call off Elenna's dragon with Torgor's red jewel! But playing a game of *Peril!* while sitting on cushions in a large, comfortable hall in King Hugo's palace wasn't much like facing real-life Avantian danger.

And that's probably a good thing, he reminded himself. *I do need some rest, after all.*

Suddenly the air above the board began to shimmer like a mirage, and a figure took shape out of nothing. It was an image of Wizard Daltec, but see-through, like a ghost.

"Hey!" said Elenna. "That's our game you're standing on."

"My apologies," said Daltec. His brow was furrowed, and Tom felt his chest tighten.

Something's wrong.

"Is everything all right?" he asked.

"I certainly hope so," said Daltec. "But I fear not. Please, you must both come to Aduro's bedchamber."

Tom and Elenna shared a glance. Aduro had been Tom's friend and

mentor through many a Quest, but
he was old and frail now. *I just hope
nothing's happened to him...*

"Of course," said Tom. "We'll come
at once."

"Hurry," said Daltec, "but don't
breathe a word of this to anyone. We

14

don't want to cause a panic."

"We'll be careful," said Elenna, rising to her feet as the image of Daltec shimmered once more, and was gone.

Together, they strode out into the Palace courtyard. A light rain was falling, pooling in puddles on the ground, and there was no one around to see them. But as Tom quickened his pace, a familiar figure appeared from a low doorway.

"Tom! Elenna!" called Captain Harkman, cheerily. He had his hood pulled up against the rain, and he was carrying a spear and shield.

Normally Tom would have been delighted to see their old friend, but Daltec's voice ran through his mind. *Don't breathe a word of this to anyone...*

"Morning, Captain," said Elenna, shooting Tom an anxious look. "Off to your training session? Don't let us keep you."

"Not at all," said Harkman. "In fact, it's you I was looking for." He paused to unleash an explosive sneeze. "At-CHOO! You see, I think I'm coming down with something. It's this awful weather." He looked at Tom with hopeful, red-rimmed eyes. "So I was wondering if you two might like to run the session – just for today."

Tom couldn't think what to say. How could he refuse the captain? But from what Daltec had said, they needed to get to Aduro's bedchamber – and quickly. He'd never seen the young Wizard look so troubled before. Could there be a new Beast threatening Avantia?

"We'd love to, of course," said Elenna, interrupting Tom's thoughts.

"But we've, er... We've got to…"

"Say no more," interrupted Captain Harkman, with a wink. "I've heard there's some leftover blackberry pie in the kitchens. I wouldn't want you to – at-CHOO! – miss out. I'll have young Westbury run the session for today. Save me a slice, eh?"

"We will," said Tom, with relief. "Get

better soon, Captain!"

"I'll certainly – at-CHOO! – try," said the captain.

They left him and hurried across the courtyard.

A narrow wooden door led to a flight of steps up to Aduro's bedchamber. As they reached the top, Tom saw that the door was wide open, and inside Daltec was standing hunched over his master's oak desk, studying a huge, leather-bound book.

The chamber was dark and quiet but for the gentle patter of rain on a small window. Dusty old tomes littered the floor and bed, and were stacked in piles against the stone walls. They made the room seem cramped, even though it was far bigger than Tom's own chamber. Yet without Aduro, it still felt empty.

"What's going on?" asked Tom, stepping over the threshold. "Where is Aduro?"

Daltec glanced up, startled from his reading. His face was pale and there were dark bags under his eyes, as though he hadn't slept a wink.

The Wizard's fingers still rested lightly on the pages of the book. One of the *Chronicles of Avantia*, Tom realised, the history of their kingdom. It was the job of the King's Wizard to keep it up to date. This was one of the more recent volumes, judging by how white the paper was. But as he peered closer, he saw that some of the pages had been ripped out of it.

"Thank goodness you're here!" said Daltec. "I called you because... well..." He sighed, and collapsed into a wooden chair. "Aduro is missing."

Tom's head snapped up, a shiver of
worry sending chills down his spine.
Aduro is missing?

"Have you tried the library?" asked
Elenna. "Or the kitchen? I've heard
there's some blackberry pie that's –"

"You don't understand," Daltec
interrupted, looking worried. "He's
been gone for two days. I've tried
using magic to find him, but there's

20

not a trace of him anywhere."

"What can that mean?" asked Tom.

"It means," said Daltec, "that my master is no longer in Avantia!"

CHAPTER TWO

MISTRESS OF THE BEASTS

Tom's heart was racing with worry, but he tried to keep his voice calm. "Let's start at the beginning," he said. "What do we know?"

"Aduro has been acting strangely for some time," said Daltec, thoughtfully. "Talking little, staying up late and hardly touching his food... Do you remember when the Tangalan ambassadors arrived, and King Hugo held a feast in their honour?"

Elenna nodded. "I didn't think anything of it at the time, but I remember now. Aduro hardly said a word all evening!"

"You're right," said Tom. "He just pushed his food around his plate. And he had been so happy about the two kingdoms communicating again. They had been enemies for years."

"Indeed," Daltec continued. "I was sure Aduro was simply tired, and that his energy would return. But then two days ago I was making a potion, and I came to ask his advice. I found his bedchamber door wide open, and he was nowhere to be seen. I've searched the palace, but I'm sure of it – he's gone."

"Does anyone else know about

this?" asked Elenna.

Daltec shook his head. "Captain Harkman was the last person to see Aduro before his disappearance. He bumped into Aduro late in the evening, looking rather flustered. According to the good captain, Aduro claimed he was heading to the stables to saddle a horse, to go and visit his niece in Spindrel."

"But that doesn't make sense," Tom interrupted. "Aduro hates riding! Especially at night."

"And even stranger," said Daltec, "I am almost positive that he doesn't have a niece in Spindrel."

Tom nodded. *It sounds as though Aduro was covering something up. But if he wasn't going to visit his niece, where has he gone?* He turned to the dusty old book that lay open on the desk.

Perhaps the answer was there, staring them in the face.

As he lifted up the front cover, Tom felt an unexpected pang of grief. It was the final volume of the *Chronicles* – the one that recorded the most recent seventy years of Avantian history. The last few written pages would tell the tale of Taladon, Tom's father, and his death at the hands of

the White Knight of Forton. Beyond that the pages would be blank, waiting for the next chapter to be written – the story of Tom's own adventures…

He blinked, forcing his thoughts back to the present. "The torn-out pages," he said. "What was on them?"

A cloud seemed to pass across Daltec's face. "The missing pages tell the tragic tale of Kara."

Tom and Elenna shared a puzzled glance. "Who's Kara?" asked Elenna.

"Allow me to show you," said Daltec. He brought his hands together, and they began to glow softly, like paper lanterns. Tendrils of white smoke snaked out from his fingertips. Elenna let out a gasp as the smoke curled into a ball that grew and grew, until it filled most of the room. Within the sphere, an image slowly formed.

It was a woman, tall and strong. She had brown eyes, fierce with determination, and her long fair hair escaped a helmet and flowed freely as though in a breeze. Her entire body was clad in gleaming gold.

Tom felt his jaw drop. "Can that be...the Golden Armour?"

"Correct," said Daltec. "Though of course the armour has changed a few times over the years. But it always carries the same magic, and each suit shapes itself to each new wearer."

"But if she's wearing the armour, she must be a Mistress of the Beasts," said Tom. "And I've never heard of her before!"

"Kara served Avantia sixty years ago," Daltec explained. "And you haven't heard of her because Aduro never mentions her name."

Tom and Elenna exchanged a glance. *Why would Aduro keep such a secret from us?*

The image of Kara shrank, and a miniature world took shape around her. She was a tiny figure now,

standing on a raft that was tossed on
a stormy sea.

"Kara was a deadly fighter," said
Daltec. "She wielded a heavy silver
axe, and was undefeated in battle.
That is, until she set sail to the island
of Krikos, for her final Beast Quest."

Tom frowned, trying to take it all in.
The raft reached a sandy shore, and
Kara jumped into the surf, pulling her

vessel up onto the beach. Beyond, a
dark, forbidding forest stretched into
the distance.

"Wait – I've heard of Krikos," said
Elenna, suddenly. "Uncle Leo says
it's a cursed place. He says all its
inhabitants went missing years ago,
but no one knows how, or why."
Elenna's face was pale in the glowing
light of Daltec's magic.

"True enough," said Daltec. "The island is cursed. For it is home to a ghostly creature..." He hesitated, as though afraid even to speak its name. "A terrible Beast called Jalka," he said at last.

A chill crept over Tom's skin as he watched the image of Kara, pulling an axe from an oilskin bag and striding into the forest. The darkness swallowed her.

All at once, the sphere of smoke melted away, and the light was gone from Daltec's hands.

"Let me guess," said Elenna. "She was never seen again?"

The Wizard nodded gravely.

Tom felt a lump form in his throat. Another brave warrior who wore the Golden Armour, and met her doom on a Beast Quest. One day, he knew, it would be his turn.

He looked up to see Elenna watching him, her brow furrowed in determination, and he felt his heart lift. *One day, but not today.*

Tom cleared his throat. "What does this have to do with Aduro?"

"An excellent question," said Daltec. "My master was just a boy when Kara disappeared. In those days he had a master of his own – the great Mivan. The old Wizard was loved and respected throughout Avantia – but he was haunted by the loss of Kara. She was not only Mistress of the Beasts...she was also Mivan's sister."

"And he never found out what happened on the island?" said Elenna.

"Alas, no," said Daltec. "Both Mivan and his young apprentice longed to discover the truth. But the great Wizard died before the mystery could be solved."

"Wait," said Tom. "Do you think Aduro could have set out to discover what really happened to Kara? But why would he do it now? He's had sixty years to solve this mystery."

"An excellent question." Daltec leafed through the pages of the book until he reached an image of a kindly old wizard. "I've been reading about Mivan," he explained. "That's him. And today is the fiftieth anniversary of his death."

"Aduro must have gone to solve the mystery," said Elenna, her eyes shining. "To honour the memory of his old master!"

"I believe so," said Daltec. "But without his magic, he will be in terrible danger. The ghost-Beast Jalka will be waiting for him. And who knows what other horrors the island of Krikos might hold..."

Tom's mind raced. Aduro had a head start – but if he really was travelling on horseback, perhaps they could catch up with him. He wasn't Avantia's finest horseman, after all. And even if it was too late – if he was already on the sea – they would never desert their old friend.

"Whatever dangers there are, we'll be ready for them," said Tom, firmly. "Don't worry, Daltec. We'll bring your master back home!"

I won't let Aduro suffer the same dreadful fate as Kara...

CHAPTER THREE

OLD FRIENDS

FFFFFZAM!

Tom's stomach lurched as thick blue smoke swirled around him, choking him and stinging his eyes.

"I don't think I'll ever get used to that," said Elenna, as the smoke finally began to clear. At her side, Silver growled, as though trying to frighten the last blue wisps away.

Tom grinned. Now that they could

see again, he found himself standing
under a grey sky on a stony beach,
windswept and empty but for him,
Elenna, Silver and Daltec. For once,
the Wizard had managed to transport
them exactly where he'd intended.

His magic is getting better all the time!

"Shall we begin?" said Daltec,

anxiously. He didn't like to use such powerful magic if he didn't have to, but they needed to catch up with Aduro, and fast. Now they were on the shore, all they needed was a way to travel to Krikos across Avantia's Western Ocean.

It's a shame Storm can't come with us, thought Tom. Normally he would never set out on a Beast Quest without his faithful stallion. But he wouldn't need him on the island of Krikos, and he knew Storm was better off in the stables of King Hugo's palace. Besides, they had Elenna's wolf Silver to keep them company.

They set out towards the sea, their footsteps sinking deep in the shingle. As they rounded a dune, Silver let out an excited bark and took off, his tail wagging as he raced ahead. In the distance, Tom saw a figure wading out of the surf, a pair of fishing rods slung over his back, pulling a dinghy with a flapping sail behind him. It was a broad-shouldered man with spiky hair and a weather-beaten face.

"Uncle Leo!" gasped Elenna. "I haven't seen him in ages!"

She sprinted after her wolf and Tom followed, leaving Daltec stumbling in their wake.

Poor Uncle Leo looked utterly bewildered at the strange group running towards him. But as they came closer, a big grin lit up his face.

"Am I dreaming?" he said. "I could swear it's my niece and her best friend, the Master of the Beasts – not to mention a certain loyal wolf and the king's Wizard!"

Elenna flung her arms round him

and hugged him tightly.

"It's so good to see you, Uncle!"

"Don't tell me," said Leo, smoothing Elenna's hair. "You're setting out on another Beast Quest, aren't you?"

Tom nodded. "And we really need to cross the Western Ocean. I wonder... Perhaps you could take us in your boat?"

"Of course!" said Leo, clapping Tom on the back so hard he winced. "Anything for you two. It's funny – I don't get a lot of visitors, but today everyone in Avantia seems to be stopping by."

"What do you mean?" said Daltec. He had only just caught up, and was panting from the run.

"Aduro," said Leo. "He was here at dawn this morning. As a matter of fact I've just got back from dropping

him off on the island of Krikos. I
don't know why anyone would want
to go there, but Wizards know best,
eh?" He winked at Daltec.

Tom noticed that the wizard had
gone very pale. "Can you take us
right now?" Tom asked.

Leo's smile disappeared as he saw
the grave expressions on their faces.

"Hop in then," he said. "We'll leave at once."

A short while later, they were riding the waves of the Western Ocean. Tom shivered as the breeze whipped across the water, buffeting the sails and rattling the rigging. Silver spotted some fish darting below the surface and growled at them, leaning so far over the edge that Elenna had to grab him and pull him back in.

"Stay in the boat, Silver," murmured Elenna, stroking her wolf to calm him down.

Tom smiled at her, but his mind was on other things. *If only this boat would go faster!* Leo's dinghy was struggling in the wind, which seemed to be blowing in a different direction every moment. Tom couldn't stop fidgeting with the leather of his sword hilt. He was certain Aduro was in terrible danger, and the sooner they arrived, the better. *After all, Krikos is the home of Jalka. The Beast who slew the mighty warrior Kara...*

"Do the *Chronicles* say anything about the Beast of Krikos?" Tom asked Daltec.

The poor Wizard was huddled on a bench, his sodden robes clinging to his body and his face tinged with green. Daltec took a deep breath and shook his head. "Not that I know of, Tom. And even if they did, those pages of the book are missing. All I can tell you is that Jalka was once called 'the ghost-Beast'."

"Jalka, did you say?" asked Uncle Leo, leaning forward from the back

44

of the boat. He held the tiller steady with one hand, while the other was busy making adjustments to the sail. "I've heard that name before. Stop off in any tavern by the shore, and you'll hear dozens of tales of the ghost-Beast. Folk say it's an evil spirit that drifts about the island, sending ships to watery graves. But I've never met anyone who's actually set foot on the island – until Aduro this morning, that is."

"Is it true?" asked Elenna.

Her uncle chuckled. "I should think not. A load of bilge if you ask me, dreamed up by old sailors who've had a drop too much grog. Of course, you'll find out for sure when you get to the island."

If we ever do get there, thought Tom, as the wind changed again, setting

the sail shuddering and flapping
against the mast.

"Hmm," said Uncle Leo.

"Is everything all right?" asked
Elenna curiously.

"It's just...the wind's all over the
place today," Uncle Leo explained.
He hesitated. "It's almost as though
something – or someone – doesn't
want us to reach Krikos... Your Jalka,
I shouldn't wonder." He grinned
at his joke. But no sooner had he
spoken than a great wave rolled up
out of nowhere, breaking against
the boat and showering them with
freezing cold spray.

"Yowch!" gasped Daltec.

Tom squirmed with frustration.
*At this rate we'll never catch up with
Aduro...* "I've got an idea," he said. He
clambered to his feet, holding onto

the mast for balance. Then he raised his shield up and touched the great sea serpent's tooth embedded in its wooden surface.

Hear me, Sepron, he thought, concentrating as hard as he could. *Avantia needs you!*

At first there was no sound but the whistling breeze, the slap of the rigging, and the lapping of waves against the hull. Then a rumbling grew, deep beneath the water.

"What in King Hugo's name…?" muttered Leo.

The next moment the surface exploded in a fountain of spray, and a mighty green head rose up, casting the dinghy into shadow. The sea serpent's scales glittered with water and its neck swayed gently, like seaweed in a current.

Tom grinned. "Uncle Leo... I think you've met Sepron before," he said.

"Y-yes," said Leo. "It hardly prepares you, though."

The Beast turned his massive head towards them.

"We need a ride," said Tom,

touching the red jewel so that Sepron would understand his request. "Can you help us?"

Sepron nodded his huge head, eyes shining with intelligence. Tom's heart swelled with excitement. Now the Quest was really starting!

CHAPTER FOUR

JUST NERVES

This is more like it! thought Tom, as Sepron cut through the waves.

He crouched on the Beast's back, grasping the sea serpent's trailing mane with one hand, while with the other he waved back at Uncle Leo. The fishing boat had almost disappeared from view now, and its sails were full. The wind seemed to have returned now that the vessel was sailing away from Krikos again.

Maybe there really is something strange about the island...

A gout of spray soaked them, and Elenna let out a joyful whoop. Sepron was swimming at top speed, and it wasn't easy to hold on. Tom's friend gripped the mane next to him, while her wolf lay flat, every muscle tense, letting out an occasional whimper when the spray hit him. Daltec seemed to be enjoying himself even less than Silver. He was on his belly, clutching at the Beast's scales, his eyes tightly shut.

"Maybe you could magic us to Krikos instead?" Tom suggested.

Daltec raised his head just enough to shake it, miserably. "Impossible – I don't know where it is! The island is said to move around the Western Ocean, disappearing and reappearing in different places."

"Just like Grashkor's prison island," said Elenna. Tom noticed that she was biting her lip, trying to stop herself from smiling at the sight of the poor Wizard clinging onto a giant sea serpent for dear life.

Suddenly Tom lost his footing and lurched forward. "Whoa there!" He grabbed onto the Beast's scales. Sepron had stopped and now drifted, still in the water.

"What's happening?" asked Elenna.

"I believe we're getting close to the island," murmured Daltec.

Tom felt a strange tingle in his belly. *Just nerves*, he told himself. But still, that was strange – ever since he had claimed the Golden Armour, its chainmail kept his heart strong in the face of any danger.

It's just because I'm worried for Aduro. The Wizard had long since lost his magic, and he was too old to be wandering around any deserted island – let alone Krikos.

How many of the old stories are true...?

Ignoring the thought, Tom drew on the power of his golden helmet and peered into the distance. Far away he could see land rising from the sea, but he couldn't make out any details.

That gave him another twinge of unease. Normally his golden helmet let him see things far away as though they were up close. Perhaps some sort of thick fog lay in his way. *Or perhaps it's the strange power of the island...*

Had Kara faced these same dangers, sixty years ago? Tom was following in her footsteps – he only hoped he wouldn't meet her fate, too.

Steeling himself, he pointed up ahead. "Land ahoy," he called.

"At last," sighed Daltec.

Tom drew on the power of his red jewel and sent a message to Sepron.

Carry on. Take us to Krikos.

After a moment, a deep voice replied, echoing inside Tom's head. It

was Sepron's voice.

Krikos is full of danger, Tom. There was another like you, many years ago. A Mistress of the Beasts. The island claimed her. If you set foot on Krikos, you might never return.

Tom concentrated hard, sending another message to the Beast.

We have no choice. We must bring back Aduro. Avantia needs him.

Finally the great serpent flicked his tail and swam cautiously on.

"Are you all right, Tom?" asked Elenna. "You look...worried."

"I'm fine," said Tom, trying to smile.

What's wrong with me? I've faced dangers like this before, haven't I?

The island loomed closer, covered in dense black forest. Waves broke over cold, grey shingle, and no creature stirred as far as the eye could see.

With every stroke of Sepron's powerful fins, the dread grew in Tom's heart. At last the Beast slowed to rest beside a half-collapsed, ramshackle wooden jetty.

"Thank you, Sepron!" called Elenna, prodding the jetty with a boot to check it was secure. She hopped off the Beast's back, followed by her wolf, his tail wagging with excitement. Tom gave Daltec a hand, helping the Wizard as he tottered onto dry land once again, then jumping onto the jetty himself.

"'Thank you', indeed," muttered Daltec. "Next time I think I'll stick to the fishing boat!"

Good luck, the voice of Sepron rumbled in Tom's mind. *I hope I will see you again…* Tom nodded to the Beast as his great green head sank below the water. Then, fighting his every instinct, he turned and paced along the jetty.

Soon they were crunching across the pebbled beach. Here and there, Tom spotted broken bits of wood jutting into the air. The remains of huts, long ago battered into ruin

by the wind and the waves. *Almost like the skeletons of houses…* It was obvious that people had lived here once, but something had driven them away. Something – or someone. Tom thought again of what Uncle Leo had said about Jalka. An evil spirit that drifts about the island, sending ships to watery graves. He'd called it a load of bilge. But here, on the island itself, Tom didn't feel so certain.

Daltec shivered, and Silver let out a whine. Even Elenna was frowning and chewing on her lip.

"Come on," said Tom, trying to sound brave for the sake of his friends. "We can't turn back now."

They strode onwards, between two towering tree trunks, and were soon walking through shadows cast by the leafy canopy of the forest. The further they went, the darker it became. The trees loomed above, so high Tom could barely see the tops of them. It was strangely quiet, as though not a single creature lived here, and their footsteps fell on nothing but dead leaves and bracken.

A low growl made Tom start, until he realised it was Silver. The wolf's hackles had risen, and he prowled close to Elenna's heels, as though he was scared to move away from her. Tom's heart was beating fast.

I'm the Master of the Beasts, he reminded himself. *I can't be afraid!*

Still, something about this Quest felt...wrong.

"Look!" called Elenna, suddenly. Tom followed her pointing finger and saw a scrap of something blue hanging from a branch up ahead.

Tom quickened his stride, hope flaring in his chest. And as he reached up to pull down the piece of material, he recognised the colour. "It's part of Aduro's cloak!"

"It must have snagged on the branch as he passed it," said Elenna. "Which means he was in a hurry."

"Perhaps he was running," murmured Tom. *But if so, what was he running from?* "Well, we're on the right track, at least. Aduro has to be somewhere on the island."

"I'm afraid you're right," said Daltec, quietly.

Elenna took the scrap of blue cloth and held it to Silver's muzzle. The wolf sniffed, getting the scent into his nostrils. Then he set off, loping fast, weaving between the trees and then bursting into a sprint.

"Yes! Go on, boy," called Elenna.

Tom followed, drawing on the power of his golden leg armour to catch up with the wolf. But he couldn't feel the magic flowing through his limbs, and the wolf streaked ahead, soon disappearing into the undergrowth.

Nothing seems right here, he thought. *Normally the Golden Armour makes me just as fast as Silver!*

Up ahead, Tom heard Silver whine.

He pushed himself as hard as he could, muscles burning as he tore through the forest, sweeping aside brambles and low-hanging branches. The trees seemed to resist him every step of the way, until suddenly he surged out into a clearing and skidded to a halt. Just ahead, the ground fell away in a steep drop. *A ravine.*

Tom gasped.

"What is it?" cried Elenna, as she came racing out of the forest behind him. Then she saw. "Oh no…"

Lying at the bottom of the ravine was a figure in a robe, sprawled out like a rag doll and completely still.

Aduro!

CHAPTER FIVE

THE MISSING PAGES

Silver let out a whimper at the sight of the fallen Wizard.

"Go on, boy," said Elenna. "See if you can find a way down. I will follow you."

As the wolf set off, prowling along the edge of the ravine, Elenna turned to Tom. "Do you think he's...?"

Tom shook his head fiercely. "No! He can't be!"

He took a step back, then launched himself out into space. At the same time he drew on the power of Arcta's eagle feather. The magic of the feather slowed his fall, until he was floating gently downwards. *At least this token actually works*, he thought as he landed in a crouch, and rushed to his old friend's side.

Aduro let out a low moan, and Tom felt relief flood his body. Slowly, carefully, he rolled the former Wizard onto his back. He looked pale, but he was alive.

"My ankle," croaked Aduro. "I think I...I might have broken it."

"Don't worry," Tom told him. "Hold still, while I heal it."

"It was my own fault," murmured Aduro, as Tom detached the green jewel from his belt, and held it to the Wizard's ankle. "I was tired, and I didn't see the ravine until...until it was too late."

"Why did you come here?" Tom asked, as the jewel began to glow with an eerie green light. "The Judge drained all your magic away, remember? You can't just set out

on a Quest like this without telling anyone. It's too dangerous!" He realised he had raised his voice, and felt a sudden flush of shame. "I'm sorry," he mumbled. "I didn't mean to get angry. It's just – we were all so worried about you."

"No, I'm sorry, Tom," said the former Wizard. The light of the jewel had faded now. Aduro flexed his ankle and clambered to his feet, brushing dead leaves and dirt from his robes. "You're absolutely right. I was a fool to come to Krikos. Can you forgive me?"

Tom smiled at his old friend fondly. "Well...I suppose so. But let's get out of here. Before you get yourself into any more trouble!"

They set off, walking side by side towards the edge of the ravine. But almost at once Aduro stopped, his hands fumbling at his robes. "Where are they?" he muttered.

"Where are what?"

Aduro looked utterly stricken. "The pages," he said. "The ones I took from the *Chronicles of Avantia*. I must have dropped them when I fell."

Tom bit his lip. He wanted nothing more than to leave Krikos as soon as possible – something about the darkness and silence of the forest made his skin crawl. But they couldn't leave behind such a valuable record of Avantian history.

I suppose we've got no choice...

"I'll try over here," Tom said, pointing to some thorny bushes nearby. "You check the rocks at the edge of the ravine."

They began looking.

Tom cast a glance up at the lip of the ravine, but his friends were nowhere to be seen. He tried to ignore it, but the dread was building again in the pit of his stomach. Where had Elenna, Silver and Daltec got to? Surely they should have found a way

down by now.

"Ah!" said Aduro, startling him. Tom whirled round and saw the Wizard hold up a handful of pages, looking a little sheepish. "They were... ahem...in my other pocket."

Tom grinned with relief.

They set out again, pushing through the foliage towards the side of the ravine, and Tom soon spotted a pathway that had been hacked through the bushes and bracken.

That must be how Elenna made her way down. But if so, she ought to have reached them by now. He quickened his stride, feeling horribly uneasy.

"Wait for me," panted Aduro. But Tom kept going.

Something's wrong. I can feel it.

The forest became thicker and darker, until every step was a struggle. At last he crested a rise and stumbled out into a clearing. Even here the overgrown grass reached up to his waist, and the forest canopy left them in shadow.

"Tom!" cried a frightened voice that was all too familiar.

On the far side of the clearing, several figures turned to glare at him. Wild-eyed men and women, dressed in filthy animal skins and armed with savage weapons made of stone. Their hair was spiked up and dyed in vivid reds and greens, and their faces were painted with intricate patterns.

But most of all Tom's gaze was fixed on the girl they'd caught, arms tied behind her back, her mouth wide open as she struggled helplessly in the grip of two large men.

"Get them off me!" yelled Elenna.

CHAPTER SIX

THE ARMOURED QUEEN

Tom was about to lunge forward when he felt a hand on his arm.

"No, Tom," warned Aduro, his voice deep and stern. "There are far too many of them."

He's right. There were at least thirty of the savage-looking people. A fight would be hopeless, even with the power of the Golden Armour to help.

At the edge of the clearing Tom noticed Daltec, his eyes wide, hands raised but hesitating as though unsure whether to unleash his magic.

At that range he might hit Elenna, thought Tom. *And even if he doesn't, she's still at their mercy.*

Hold on... Where's Silver?

Tom scanned the long grass, but he couldn't see the wolf anywhere. Had they captured him? Killed him?

No – he was being foolish. Silver was far too quick to be caught by men on foot. *Don't get distracted.*

Tom stepped forward, holding out his hands.

"Please, we mean no harm," he said. He pointed at Aduro. "We only came here to bring our friend home. If you let us go, we'll leave you in peace."

One of the wild figures stepped

forward – a towering, well-muscled
man, with a long dirty beard and
tangled green hair that reached almost
to his waist. He wore a rough-spun
brown tunic and a belt made of twisted
vines, from which dangled a heavy
stone warhammer.

"You lie," growled the man. His
face was covered in black swirls of
paint that made him look even more

frightening. "You brought a monster among us, with filthy fur and savage teeth. We drove it away."

"What monster?" said Tom, bewildered. *Does he mean Silver?*

There was an eerie hissing from the wild figures.

"Again you lie!" said the bearded man. "All strangers lie! The Armoured Queen told us this."

"Hail the Armoured Queen!" roared one of the women.

"Hail!" the others answered.

"You have come here to take our island for yourselves," said the bearded man, his eyes narrowed. "It is just as our queen warned us!"

The Armoured Queen. Tom felt a strange, dizzy sensation as he heard the name. He had a nasty feeling he knew who that was... But it couldn't be possible, could it?

"People of Krikos," said Aduro, stepping forward. "I am a historian of Avantia. Where I come from, it is believed that you were all swept away by terrible storms. But I see now you have simply become cut off and isolated from the rest of the realm. I can assure you that not all strangers have wicked intentions. I myself –"

"Silence!" howled the bearded man. "Do you think we are children? We shall not trust the false tongue of an invader, however ancient he may be. We know of such deceptions, thanks to the –"

"The Armoured Queen?" interrupted Elenna. "I'd like a word with her!"

"Perhaps we could offer you something in exchange for letting us go," suggested Tom. "Is there anything

that you need?"

"Enough!" snarled the bearded
man. "You are trying to trick us
again. In the name of the Armoured
Queen...take them prisoner!"

Before Tom could react, six men
rushed forward, levelling stone-
tipped spears at him, Daltec and

Aduro. *Trapped.* He caught Elenna's
eye, and she raised one eyebrow in an
unspoken question.

How are we getting out of this?

Tom only wished he knew.

CHAPTER SEVEN

KARA'S FATE

The islanders herded them to the edge of the clearing.

A burly man yanked Tom's arms upwards and tied his wrists to a low-hanging branch, using cords made from twisted vines. Tom's mind was racing. *We have to escape somehow!* But the cords were thick and strong, and with the powers of his armour failing him, he knew he couldn't just snap them.

As the islander stepped away, Tom found he had to stand on tiptoe or risk losing his grip on the branch. To his left, he saw Elenna and Daltec being lashed to neighbouring branches. To his right, poor Aduro was struggling to get his arms up high enough.

"Leave him alone!" Tom cried. "Can't you see he's just an old man?"

But their captors ignored him as they tied the former Wizard's wrists to the branch and left him dangling like a puppet.

The big, bearded islander watched warily, while his companions made a pile of weapons – Tom's sword and shield and Elenna's bow and arrows. They muttered to one other in low voices, casting occasional glances at their captives. Tom spotted one of them draw a finger across his throat, then spit on the ground.

That doesn't look good...

"What do you think you're doing?" demanded Elenna. Even tied up and helpless, she sounded defiant.

"Be quiet!" snapped the bearded man. "It is not for me to decide your fate. It is for the Armoured Queen!"

"Who is this Queen?" asked Tom. "Could we speak to her? Perhaps if –"

The bearded man crossed the clearing in three great bounds and grabbed Tom by his throat. The big fingers squeezed, and Tom let out a gurgle at the pressure. Up close the man smelled of smoke and sweat.

"Do not speak of our Queen again, stranger," he hissed. His eyes blazed with fury. "You are not worthy even to utter her name."

All at once the fingers let go, leaving Tom choking for breath as the bearded man strode back to his companions.

"Daltec," murmured Elenna. "Can't you cast some kind of spell to get us out of this?"

The Wizard shook his head sadly. "I fear that would be unwise. In cultures such as these, magic is often feared and hated beyond reason. If I were to reveal myself as a wizard, they might kill us all on the spot."

"Well, I'm out of ideas," said Elenna. "What about you, Tom?" She and Daltec both looked at him.

They're counting on me, thought Tom, and panic surged through his body at the thought.

Something was wrong – really wrong. He should be fighting his way to freedom, but instead he was hesitating, frightened of a few men and women armed with primitive stone weapons.

He was ashamed to admit it, but he didn't have a choice. "I can't understand it," he said. "I know I should be doing something but I'm...I'm afraid."

Elenna's eyebrows shot up. "Afraid?"

Tom turned to Aduro, his cheeks burning. "What does it mean?" he asked. "Is it something to do with the island of Krikos?"

Aduro's brow was creased with worry as he shook his head.

"I think not. It is most curious... In all of Avantian history, I have never read of a Master of the Beasts losing his nerve. Perhaps –"

He broke off, and Tom saw that his eyes were wide as he stared at something across the clearing. He followed his old friend's gaze.

An islander had just entered the clearing, carrying a heavy double-headed axe on a cushion made out of woven leaves. The bearded man took it gently, as though terrified of

damaging it. The twin silver blades
flashed in a ray of sunshine.

Something stirred in Tom's memory.
*A silver axe... Where have I heard of a
silver axe before?*

"You!" bellowed Aduro, startling
Tom from his thoughts. His friend was
leaning forward as far as his bonds
would let him, glaring furiously at the

bearded man. "How dare you touch that? It doesn't belong to you!"

The bearded man's face went red with a rage to match Aduro's.

"You accuse me of theft? You, who seek to invade our island? This axe has belonged to Krikos since before I was born. It is the weapon of our Armoured Queen!"

"It is the weapon of Kara!" Aduro growled back at him.

Tom had never seen his old friend look so angry before. The big islander could have crushed Aduro's skull with a single fist, but he didn't seem to care. "She was Mistress of the Beasts," Aduro declared. "A great warrior from the Kingdom of Avantia. My master, Mivan, enchanted the axe with his own hands!"

Of course! thought Tom,

remembering the vision Daltec had shown him of the tall woman with flowing fair hair and brown eyes, and her silver axe – the same axe the bearded man was holding now.

The islander glowered fiercely. "It is time you paid for your insolence," he said, hefting the weapon. "Prepare yourself, old trickster. You shall be the first to taste the Queen's axe."

Tom's heart raced. *I can't let him hurt Aduro!*

Swallowing his fears, he tensed his muscles and tugged at the vines that held his wrists. But the vines held.

What's happening? Normally the golden breastplate gives me incredible strength...

Suddenly he understood.

"It's not working!" he muttered.

"What's not working?" said Elenna.

"The Golden Armour! That's why

I'm afraid. And that's why I don't have my usual speed, or my strength. Ever since we came to this island, it's as though its powers have been blocked somehow."

"But if that's true," said Daltec, "what could be blocking them?"

A sudden hush fell over the clearing. From the forest, footsteps could be heard – heavy ones, crushing foliage and branches. The bearded man froze and lowered the axe, as the islanders all turned as one.

Tom felt his jaw drop, and heard sharp intakes of breath from his three friends at the same time.

A woman had stepped into the clearing – but no ordinary woman. She seemed to be two people trapped in a single body. Her left side was that of a tall, strong warrior with long

hair, dressed in gleaming armour.
Tom recognised her at once – it was
Kara, Mistress of the Beasts, and she
looked as though she hadn't aged a
day. But her right side was that of
a strange, ghostly creature, its body
formed out of thick blue smoke, its

one eye dark and menacing.

The two halves seemed to be squirming, trying to pull apart from each other, and it was only a shining golden breastplate that held them together. She must have lost her battle with Jalka – and suffered a fate worse than death.

Tom's mind was racing. Kara's battle-gear looked just like his own – an earlier version of the Golden Armour. *That's why my powers are failing me*, he realised. *On this island, Kara's suit still has the magic...*

Aduro let out a low moan. "It can't be," he muttered. "Kara...what have they done to you?"

Through the Red Jewel of Torgor, Tom heard two voices speaking as one – the voice of a young woman, and a whispering hiss that made his skin crawl. Both spoke the same words.

Avantia's heroine is no more. Jalka the ghost-Beast is no more. Now there is only me...Jakara!

STORY TWO

How could I have been so foolish?

In my haste to find my master Aduro, I have allowed us all to stray into fatal danger. The Island of Krikos holds terrors greater than I could ever have imagined. Not only the fierce islanders, hostile to all who land on their shores. But, worse, their Armoured Queen…Jakara. She is a foul union of the ghostly Jalka and Kara, who served as Mistress of the Beasts many years ago.

Worse still, the Beast wears Kara's Golden Armour. It is sapping the magic from Tom's own suit of armour, leaving him – and us – defenceless.

Whatever it takes, we must defeat the Beast, and save poor Kara from her hideous fate.

I only wish I knew how…

Daltec

Wizard of Avantia

CHAPTER ONE

WHAT FEAR FEELS LIKE

"Hail, Armoured Queen!" roared the leader of the islanders.

"Hail!" the others replied. They fell to their knees in a circle around the edge of the clearing, as their ruler bowed his head and offered up the silver axe.

Jakara's lips curled in a sinister, lopsided smile as she took the weapon in her left hand, lifting it effortlessly and slicing it through the air in a practice stroke.

Tom's cheeks flushed with anger at the sight of the Armoured Queen wielding a weapon that belonged to a Mistress of the Beasts. But he couldn't do a thing about it – the cords around his wrists held him firmly in place.

"These lying strangers have come to invade our island, Your Majesty," said the bearded man. "We have bound them for you, ready for their punishment."

The Beast turned her gaze on Aduro, her dark right eye glimmering. She hefted her axe as she advanced.

Come on, Tom told himself. *Do something!* He didn't have the powers of the Golden Armour, but he had defeated Beasts without them before.

Use your wits, Tom.

He craned his neck to peer at the tree trunk behind him. There had to be something he could use... Soon he saw a spot above his head, where a branch had snapped off to leave nothing but a sharp, stubby bit of wood behind.

But is it sharp enough?

Jakara's voice hissed in his head. *It is long since my axe has tasted blood. This old man should count it an honour.*

Summoning all his strength, Tom sprang upwards, jumping and twisting in the air so that as he fell, the vines scraped against the jagged shard of wood.

SNAP!

His bonds broke, and he collapsed to his knees.

"Yes!" shouted Elenna. "Well done,

Tom. Now get her!"

"The boy is free!" yelled an islander. "Catch him, quick!"

Tom rose shakily, his muscles aching from the impact of the fall. Jakara had seen him, and with a snarl she turned and closed in faster on Aduro, her silver axe gleaming...

The nearest islander lunged towards Tom, but he dodged easily aside and darted forward.

His limbs tingled with adrenaline. *So this is what fear feels like...* He'd almost forgotten before he came to Krikos. But now he drew on its energy, turning it into a speed and strength born of desperation. Before any of the islanders could stop him, he reached the pile of weapons and snatched up his sword and shield. The bearded man with long green hair stepped in front of him, tugging his stone warhammer free. Tom swerved away and leapt at Jakara.

While there's blood in my veins, you won't hurt my friends!

The Beast clearly heard him coming, because she spun to face him. Tom had to skid to a halt as the silver axe whistled above him with sickening speed. Any lower, and it

would have taken off his head. He crouched into a fighting stance, just as Jakara swung her axe a second time.

The impact almost tore his arm from the socket. It sent him staggering back, halfway across the clearing. Hands grabbed him from behind and he overbalanced, falling as the islanders piled onto him, pinning him firmly to the ground.

Tom gritted his teeth and struggled, but without the strength of the golden breastplate, he couldn't resist for long. Looking over an islander's shoulder, he could just see Jakara turn back to Aduro and lift her axe a second time...

"No!" howled Elenna, as she tugged at her bonds.

Daltec said nothing, paralysed by shock, as Aduro looked the Beast squarely in her mismatched eyes and spoke calmly. "I forgive you, Kara, and I am sorry for your fate," he said. "You do not know what has become of you."

Tom couldn't bear to watch. He closed his eyes...

...as a sound burst through the forest – a savage but familiar sound. The urgent howl of a wolf. Tom's eyelids flicked open again, and he saw that the islanders were exchanging horrified glances.

"It's coming back," said one, fearfully. "The invaders' monster!"

The next moment Elenna's wolf burst into the clearing, teeth bared, fur bristling.

Silver!

The wolf launched himself at the closest group of islanders, snarling with wild fury. Screams filled the air

and Tom's captors let go, scrambling over each other in their desperate hurry to escape.

Tom staggered to his feet. He raised his sword and shield as he turned to the centre of the clearing, and faced the Beast that stood looming over his old wizard friend.

Come on then, Jakara. Let's see what you've got!

CHAPTER TWO

GHOSTFIRE!

"Silver!" cried Elenna. "Here, boy!"
The wolf let out a whine at the
sight of his mistress and raced up
to her, jumping and chewing at her
bonds. Silver would free Elenna soon
enough.

*I can trust them to look after Aduro and
Daltec,* Tom told himself. He focussed
his attention on Jakara, adjusting his
grip on his sword hilt. The Beast spun

to face him, twirling her axe so fast it blurred. The human half of her body was tensed, ready to spring, while her blue, ghostly arm trailed mist as she beckoned with one finger.

Tom threw himself forward, shield raised, swinging his sword with all the strength he could muster. The Beast snarled and met the blow with her axe.

Clang! The impact jarred Tom's arm. But as he darted away again, he saw that Jakara was stumbling backwards.

Maybe I'm stronger than I thought… Or has the strength of the Armour returned to me?

If so, there was no time to wonder why. Tom twisted, throwing his weight into a lunge. But this time Jakara was ready. She let his blade

scrape off her axe and stepped in
close, reaching for Tom with the
hand made of blue mist.

Tom drew in a sharp breath as the

hand passed straight into his chest. It was like a shard of ice, stabbing into his body and freezing his insides.

Jakara smiled as Tom choked, unable to move.

The cold seemed to creep through

his blood, until he could barely feel anything else. It crawled higher, from his chest into his neck, his face, his head... And then came a sudden anger, and a strange thought pushed its way into his mind.

They will all bow to us! All the people of Krikos. Just as soon as we are complete...

Somehow he knew that the thought wasn't his own.

It's the Beast – she's trying to make me part of her, just like Kara!

Jakara was deadly enough as it was, but if a second Master of the Beasts were to become part of her... *I can't let it happen.* Drawing on every ounce of his willpower, Tom forced his sword arm to move, and sent the blade slicing through Jakara's ghostly right arm. The Beast let out a terrible howl of fury.

In an instant all the coldness drained from Tom's body. He ducked as Jakara struck again with her axe. Almost at once, the Beast's severed, wispy limb grew back, tendrils of blue mist forming a new arm, hand and fingers. Jakara's double face twisted in another savage smile.

Tom stole a quick glance across

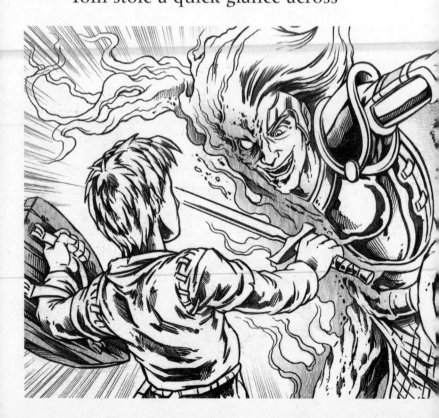

the clearing, and saw that Silver had
gnawed through all the vines holding
his friends captive. While Daltec and
Aduro rubbed at their wrists, Elenna
snatched up her bow and fitted an
arrow to the string.

"Back off, Jakara!" she roared, as
she let fly. The arrow glanced off
the Beast's golden breastplate with a

sound like a beaten gong, and Jakara stumbled away. Elenna had already fitted another arrow, and loosed it after the first. *Whhhhshh!* It passed straight through the ghostly half of the Beast. With a howl of anguish, Jakara took another step back, just as Elenna nocked a third arrow...

"Wait!" yelled Tom. At the edge of the clearing, the islanders were reappearing through the trees, creeping forward with their weapons raised and their eyes darting in every direction. It seemed as though they had managed to overcome their fear of Silver.

They might have taken us prisoner, but we can't risk hurting them with those arrows. It wouldn't be right.

Elenna froze, unsure what to do, as Jakara turned her hideous eyes on them and lifted her axe once more...

"Ghostfire!" came a cry from Aduro.

What does he mean?

But the next moment Tom understood, as Daltec stepped forward and flung out his hands, murmuring an incantation under his breath. At once, flames surged into life all around them. The whole clearing lit up in red and orange.

"Forest fire!" yelled someone.

"Run for your lives!" cried another frightened voice.

It's a spell, Tom guessed. *An illusion to stop the islanders from attacking. Aduro still has a trick or two up his sleeve!* But there was no time to congratulate the old man and his former apprentice for saving them.

"Let's get out of here!" Tom shouted, leading the way as he cut

119

a path through the forest with his sword. As he turned to check that his friends were following, he caught a glimpse of Jakara's face, glaring at

him through the flames.

She'll be after us soon enough, thought Tom. *And she'll want revenge...*

CHAPTER THREE

KARA'S CHOICE

They ran until they came to a hollow overhung by thick foliage. It was gloomy and deadly quiet. *That's good,* thought Tom. *It means the islanders aren't following us.*

Aduro stumbled to a halt, wheezing and panting. "At last," he gasped.

"Don't worry, we're safe now," Tom told him. It was painful to see his old friend so exhausted. Tom gathered some moss together to form a makeshift cushion, and settled Aduro down on it.

Meanwhile Elenna crouched, peering over the lip of the hollow, her wolf at her side. After a while she nodded. "I think we're safe. I can't hear a thing."

"What a relief!" murmured Daltec, mopping his brow with a handkerchief.

All the same, Tom felt a twinge of unease. *We're not running*, he told himself. *We're playing for time. There has to be a way to defeat Jakara.*

He just wasn't sure what it was.

Maybe it would be better to leave now. They'd rescued Aduro, after all. They could make a break for the coast, call on Sepron the Sea Serpent to take them back to Avantia, and never return to Krikos…

Tom shook himself to clear his head. He knew it was his fear talking, a fear silenced for so long by the Golden Armour. But with or without its magic, he was still a Master of the Beasts. He couldn't leave Kara behind. She had already suffered for sixty years, and he wouldn't turn his back on her now.

"We've got to defeat Jakara," he said, his voice steely with determination. "But how?"

"Maybe we could use Silver?" suggested Elenna. "Those islanders were terrified of him!"

Aduro held up a finger as he caught his breath. "Perhaps," he said. "But I suspect they were only afraid because they have never seen a creature like Silver on Krikos. Most animals appear to have abandoned the island years ago. Kara, on the other hand, has seen wolves before – your friend would hold no fear for her."

Silver whined in protest, and Elenna knelt at his side. "I think you're frightening. And you were really clever to jump out at them like that!" She scratched Silver behind his

ears, and the wolf let out a soft growl of pleasure.

"I've been thinking," said Tom. "While I was fighting Jakara, there was a moment when I felt like my strength came back – just for an instant..."

"Aha!" said Daltec. "I wondered if it might be so. I suspect that the power of the Golden Armour is passing back and forth between you and Jakara. The magic is only sufficient to serve one suit at a time. Here on Krikos there are two suits. Hence the magic is trying to serve you both."

"So my armour might work some of the time," said Tom. "Well, I suppose it's a start."

"Wait," said Elenna, her brow creased in thought. "If the magic is serving Kara as well as Tom, that

must mean there's some good in her.
So if we could get through to her
somehow…"

"…perhaps she could help us, even
from inside the Beast," finished Tom.

"Perhaps," agreed Daltec.

Tom nodded. Then, taking a deep
breath, he drew on Torgor's red jewel
to speak to the Beast.

Where are you, Jakara?

Almost at once, twin voices erupted
inside his head, howling furiously
at each other. On one hand was the
voice of Kara, determined and brave.
On the other was the voice of Jalka,
hissing with malevolence.

I'm inside the mind of Jakara, Tom
realised. He fought to suppress a
surge of fear. *That means the Beast is
close by…*

A vision began to swirl in front of

his mind's eye. Two figures locked in deadly combat – a tall, fair-haired woman wearing the Golden Armour and wielding a silver axe, and a strange, shadowy Beast formed from blue mist. Every time the Beast lunged, a fierce wind buffeted Kara, sending her stumbling.

It's a memory, he realised. *A memory of a battle that took place sixty years ago. The battle between Kara and Jalka.*

As Tom watched, Kara leapt forward into an attack, nimble as a dancer. Her axe hummed through the air, so fast Tom could barely follow its movements. But Jalka was every bit as quick, dodging the blow in a trail of blue smoke. The Beast lashed out with a limb, and hurled Kara against a tree. As she dropped to the ground, Tom saw a broken branch, dripping with blood. *She's injured…badly.*

With a jolt Tom found that he could actually feel their emotions – the spiteful rage of the Beast mingling with the righteous anger of Avantia's brave heroine.

It was Jalka's turn to attack now, raking with its claws and forcing Kara to stagger backwards, out of

range. Tom could tell from her weak movements and the way she gripped her side that she was shielding a terrible injury.

The Mistress of the Beasts hesitated a moment, then unstrapped her golden breastplate and left it flapping at her side. Tom wanted to scream at Kara – what in all Avantia was she

doing? But inside their combined mind, he was just a helpless spectator.

Quick as a darting snake, Jalka lunged forward again and slashed at Kara's exposed body with its claws. Tom winced, remembering the hideous, icy feeling when the Beast had struck him with its ghostly hand.

The next moment Kara seized hold of Jalka and pulled the ghost-Beast close to her. She wrapped both of them up in her golden breastplate and fastened it tight.

Tom felt sick as he watched the two figures squirm in agony, and become one...

Jakara.

Half woman, half Beast.

It was Kara's only choice, he realised. She was the Mistress of the Beasts, and she couldn't defeat Jalka –

so she joined herself to her opponent.
To carry out her duty, Kara had been
forced to make the ultimate sacrifice.
Tom could only imagine the horror
of being chained to such an evil
creature for sixty years, trying to fight
its wicked will and stop the Beast

hurting any more people.

The vision melted away like snow in sunshine, and he realised that Elenna was shaking him. "Tom! What's wrong?"

His friends were all looking at him in alarm.

"You cried out," said Daltec. "As though you had seen something terrible."

"You could say that..." said Tom. "But I'll explain later. First we need to get out of here, before –"

There was a thunderous rending sound from nearby, and they all turned to see an uprooted tree come crashing down the slope towards them, snapping branches and sending leaves fluttering in all directions. The next moment a tall figure appeared at the edge of the hollow, glaring down at them, its silver axe catching the ragged rays of sunshine that passed through the forest canopy above.

Jakara!

CHAPTER FOUR

FACING FEAR

"Run!" shouted Elenna.

Tom jerked into action. He turned and raced across the hollow, footsteps crunching dead leaves, as he and his friends fled the towering figure of the Beast. Glancing back, Tom saw their enemy step slowly and deliberately down into the hollow. Her Golden Armour clanked as she hefted her axe. Her hair streamed out behind

her, and a savage light danced in her
mismatched eyes.

Aduro was puffing and panting to
keep up, and Tom reached down to
pull his old friend up and over the
edge of the hollow. As he did so, he
saw tendrils of mist drifting from
the ghostly half of Jakara's body,
stretching out like spectral fingers to

clutch at them. It sent a fresh tingle of fear down his spine.

We've got to get out of here, and fast!

Tom brought up the rear as they hurried into the dense forest, out of sight of the Beast. But the blue mist pursued them like a fog, seeping through the branches. Aduro coughed and stumbled, and Tom bent again to help the old man. Without thinking he drew the strange mist into his lungs, and his chest throbbed with a sudden icy cold. His head felt light, and he swayed.

"Tom!" It was Elenna's voice, but he barely heard it. The voices of Jalka and Kara sounded in his head again. Except this time they weren't arguing, as before. Instead they spoke as one, eerily harmonised.

Face me, Tom. I am Jakara, and this

day I shall claim a second Master of the Beasts. Prepare yourself for the highest of all honours... For once you are part of me, we shall be invincible!

Tom spluttered, forcing the blue mist from his body.

Not today, Jakara, he swore. *Not today, and not ever!*

"Hurry, Tom!" called Daltec from up ahead. "The Beast will catch you!"

Tom hesitated. He closed his eyes, summoning up all his courage before he opened them again. "Then let it," he said.

They all turned to gape at him. Even Silver cocked his head and let out a confused whimper.

"What are you talking about, Tom?" asked Elenna. "If we don't go now –"

"Not we," said Tom, trying to make his voice sound calmer than he felt.

140

"You must go – get Daltec and Aduro to safety. But I can't run, no matter how much I want to. I'm a Master of the Beasts! So what if I don't have the powers of my Golden Armour? I still have to protect the kingdom. I have to face my fears."

Elenna set her jaw. "Then I'll face them with you."

"And I shall too," said Aduro, still wheezing from the effort of the run.

Daltec looked nervous for a moment before he nodded, firmly. "Very well, then. Together."

Tom's heart swelled to see his friends smiling at him, every one of them as determined as he was.

"Just promise me you'll stay out of danger," he told them.

Elenna opened her mouth to argue, but before she could speak, Tom turned, drew his sword and rushed back to the hollow.

The Beast was waiting there, still and silent, as though she had known he would come back. When she saw him, her face split in a cruel smile, and her axe glittered, razor-sharp, in her hand.

Tom felt adrenaline flood his limbs as he scrambled down into the hollow. But it was no good running now. They faced each other, like contestants in a fighting arena.

I'm ready, Jakara!

Tom lifted his shield, his heart pounding.

We shall see, hissed the voice of Jakara in Tom's head. The next moment she struck, lunging with her ghostly arm. Tom deflected the blow with his shield and slashed his sword, forcing Jakara to dance aside.

They circled each other, as Tom tried to plan his next move. He knew this wasn't going to be easy. *Jalka's arm is every bit as deadly as Kara's axe!* Still, even without the Golden Armour, he had his jewelled belt...

Quickly, Tom drew on the power of the amber jewel. The magic surged into his sword arm, improving his skill with the weapon tenfold. He leapt forward and took a lightning-fast swing at his opponent's axe. *Clang!* With a flash of silver, the weapon sailed out of Jakara's hand and landed head-first in the undergrowth nearby. Tom rolled towards it, sheathed his sword and slung his shield on his back. Then he tugged the axe free.

His muscles burned with the effort.

It's so heavy! If only I had the strength of the golden breastplate to help me... But he had nothing except his wits and his determination. Gradually he lifted the weapon, turning on Jakara.

The Beast let out a growl of fury.

"Come on, Tom!" yelled a voice

from above. It was Elenna, standing with Silver, Daltec and Aduro at the lip of the hollow. The sight fired Tom's heart. Swallowing his fear, he swung the axe. Jakara took a step back. He swung again, and again the Beast retreated.

It's working!

Heart racing, Tom forced the Beast back across the hollow, until she was snarling with her back to the slope.

"You've got her!" cried Daltec. "Hurrah!"

Tom raised his axe again...

"Stop!"

It was a new voice. Glancing upwards, Tom saw that a host of figures had appeared, silhouetted at the lip of the hollow on the opposite side from his friends. His heart sank.

The islanders. There were even more

than before, and they carried stone
spears, axes and swords of their own.

"Turn back, please!" Tom called to
them. "Can't you see, this Beast is
dangerous?"

The bearded, muscular islander
who had taken them prisoner before
stepped forward. Angrily, he pointed

a spear at Tom.

"You dare to call our Armoured Queen a Beast? You shall die!"

CHAPTER FIVE

NOWHERE TO RUN

Whhhshhhh! THUNK!

A spear launched by an islander embedded itself in the ground beside Tom's foot. He took a step backwards as an axe whirred past, striking a tree trunk on the far side of the hollow with a dull thud.

If Jakara doesn't kill me, these islanders will!

"Please," he tried again. "It's her

you should be fighting, not me!"
But from their fierce glares, he could
tell it was hopeless. Jakara stepped
forward with new purpose shining in
her strange eyes.

Somewhere behind him he heard
Elenna's voice again.

"Daltec, can't you do something?"
The next moment the Wizard's

voice rang out, chanting strange,
mystical words that Tom had never
heard before.

There was a humming sound,
and the air seemed to shimmer as
something took shape above Tom
– a dome of faint red light that
covered the hollow like a canopy,
sealing Tom and Jakara inside it and

throwing a sinister blood-red shadow over their battle.

Tom breathed a sigh of relief as he saw the islanders back away from the dome, their eyes wide, clearly terrified of the Wizard's magic. Now they couldn't help their Armoured Queen. But on the other hand, Tom had nowhere to run...

Just you and me now, little Master of the Beasts, spoke the double voice of Jakara inside his mind. *Are you afraid?*

Tom shook his head, ignoring the squirm of fear in his belly. He gripped the silver axe tighter and reached out with his mind, challenging the Beast. If he could make her angry, perhaps she might make a mistake...

It's you who should be afraid, Tom

told her. *You're unarmed, and I'm much stronger than that weakling Kara ever was. I'm more than a match for a freak like you!*

Jakara let out an unearthly howl of fury. *You will pay for your insolence!*

The Beast lunged forward, snatching hold of the axe shaft

before Tom could pull it out of her reach. His muscles tensed as he fought against her, trying to hold onto the axe. Jakara hissed and tried to tug it away from him.

All at once Tom felt the magic of the golden breastplate leak out of him and swell Jakara's strength. The next moment she tore the axe from his grasp and lashed out with a high kick that caught Tom on the jaw, sending him spinning away. He tumbled to the ground and his shield came loose, the edge of it catching his stomach hard.

Winded, Tom gasped for air as he shook the shield free and turned onto his back. His feet scrabbled in the dirt as he pushed himself backwards across the leafy ground, towards the edge of the glowing red dome that Daltec had conjured.

His jaw throbbed with pain. *Now I
know what it's like being on the receiving
end of that strength!* It hurt more than
he could possibly have imagined.
But he couldn't give up now. Jakara
was stalking towards him, whirling
the axe with such speed it became a
great silver blur.

Tom's fear surged up again, threatening to overwhelm him. But at the last minute he leapt to his feet, dodging just in time as the axe swept past. He felt the breeze ruffle his hair. Jakara swung again and he somersaulted backwards, ending up right at the edge of the hollow, where the red light of the dome met the ground. Above him, the islanders had found their courage and were striking at the magical dome with axes and spears, sending booming vibrations across it as they tried to break through. But Daltec's magic held firm. Tom knew if the islanders attacked Daltec, the spell would be broken. But the wild men and women were focused on their queen, their only thought to bash down the force-field that contained her.

Tom looked up and already Jakara was on him again, raising her axe double-handed over her head for one last, fatal blow. Through the dark-red shimmering surface of the dome, Tom caught a glimpse of Elenna mouthing something.

Go back.

It took him a moment to understand. *Of course!*

He scrambled away, getting as close as he could to the lip of the hollow, as Jakara descended on him. She brought her axe whistling down.

Tom closed his eyes. *This is it. Just don't move a muscle...*

CLANNGG!

Jakara was too close to the edge of the dome. Her axe struck the underside of it, sending the weapon juddering out of her hands.

Now's my chance! Tom tugged his sword from its scabbard and darted forward. Everything depended on this one, single move. He swung, aiming for the leather straps that held Jakara's breastplate in place. *Whhhhsh!* The blade sliced clean through, and the breastplate

clattered to the ground. Jakara's
anguished cry filled Tom's mind.

Noooo!

CHAPTER SIX

THE FINAL BLOW

There was a sound like rushing wind
and a blinding flash of light, and Tom
threw his arms up to cover his eyes.
When he looked again, he saw that
Jakara had fallen to her knees. No –
not the Beast. A tall woman with long
blonde hair...

Kara!

Whole again at last, and still
clutching her silver axe.

Above her floated a cloud of blue
mist that swirled in the rough shape
of a person, its eyes burning black
with fury. Jalka the Ghost Beast.

They've split in two!

Kara lifted her head and blinked, as
though unsure where she was. Then
her lips curled into a smile and she
rose to her feet, twirling the silver axe

with deadly speed.

"You don't know how long I've waited for this," she told Tom, with a wink. "Are you with me? Let's defeat this Beast, once and for all."

Tom nodded. Together they turned to face Jalka.

The Beast hissed and swooped across the hollow as it tried to escape. But Daltec's dome of magic sealed them in on all sides.

Kara struck first, swinging her axe every bit as fast as Jakara had. The spectral blue figure ducked out of range, but it gave Tom the chance to lunge with his sword. Jalka darted away, slower this time. Trapped by the dome, there was no way the Beast could escape.

Jalka's voice hissed inside Tom's head. *This battle is unequal. Face me one at a time, or not at all!*

Tom thought of Kara, trapped for so many years alongside this hideous Beast. An eternity without hope – and yet she had never given up. His heart hardened, and his grip tightened on the hilt of his sword.

"I'll show you all the mercy you deserve," said Tom. He hacked at Jalka's neck, putting all his strength behind it.

But once again the Beast slipped away, and Tom's blade swept through nothing but thin air. *This is just like fighting smoke!*

Jalka let out an eerie screech. *It's laughing,* Tom realised.

So be it, said the Beast's voice in his head. *You had your chance, Tom. Now prepare to die!*

The Beast lunged suddenly with

both hands, blue fingers trailing
smoke, icy cold as they clutched
Tom's throat and began to squeeze...

Can't...breathe...

It happened so fast Tom barely saw
it. Kara stepped in, whirling her axe
above her head then down, like a

butcher's cleaver on a chopping block.

"Farewell, Jalka," she roared.

WHHHHHSSSH!

The silver blade glowed with a strange light as it sliced through Jalka from its head to its toes, burying itself in the ground with a dull thud.

Jalka howled as its body split in

two with a rushing, searing sound. It was so loud that Tom had to drop his sword and clap his hands tightly over his ears.

He watched, stunned, as the two halves of the Beast melted away until there was nothing left but a whirling breeze that stirred the leaves, and

then was still. Even afterwards the howl lingered, chilling Tom's blood.

Jalka was no more.

When there was silence at last, the dome of red light flickered, then disappeared altogether, letting the sunshine in once again.

Daltec fell to his knees. He wrung his hands, pale with exhaustion at the effort of keeping up the spell for such a long time.

Tom tensed as he remembered the islanders. *In a moment we'll have another battle on our hands!* But as he turned to face them, sword raised, he saw that they had dropped their weapons. They were blinking and rubbing their eyes, as though they'd only just woken up.

"What...what's happening?" said one of the islanders.

"Where are we?" said another.

Aduro hitched up his robes and stepped down into the hollow, his kind old face beaming with happiness. "Jakara's hold over the islanders is broken," he explained. "You've rescued them, Tom!"

"It wasn't me," said Tom, quickly. "It was Kara who struck the final blow. She saved us."

The Mistress of the Beasts was leaning heavily on her axe, bent over and panting, as though exhausted by the fight. She caught Tom's eye, and smiled at him.

"What was that terrible noise at the end?" asked Elenna. She was kneeling beside Silver, running soothing hands through his fur. The wolf was trembling.

"Ah yes," said Aduro. "Jalka's

screech is truly deafening."

For a few moments no one spoke.

Then at last the silence was broken
by a low groan. Tom spun round to
see that Kara had collapsed to her
knees again, head bowed, her axe
fallen.

When Kara looked up, Tom gasped
in shock. A thin line of red ran

from the corner of her mouth, and one hand was pressed against her stomach...

It was covered in blood.

CHAPTER SEVEN

THE GALLERY OF TOMBS

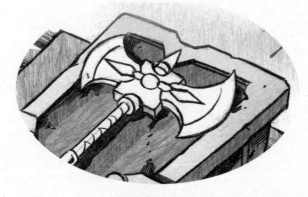

"Kara!" yelled Tom. His heart lurched as he saw the Mistress of the Beasts slump to the ground, breathing heavily. *After everything we've been through... We have to save her!* He rushed to kneel at her side.

"Let me see," demanded Elenna, as she came running and skidded to her knees next to them. "Aduro, what herbs are there on the island? There must be something that can help."

"There's my shield!" said Tom. "I'll use the talon of Epos."

But as he reached to pull the healing talon from the wood, he felt a strong hand on his. Kara's hand. Smiling a sad smile, the Mistress of the Beasts shook her head.

"No, young master. This wound cannot be healed." Her voice was soft and gentle, now that she was free of the Beast.

Tom turned to Aduro, but the old man's face was grave, and he remained silent.

"Of course it can," snapped Elenna. "Don't be foolish! If you'll just let us we can –"

"No," said Kara, more firmly this time. "You don't understand. Jalka

gave me this injury sixty years ago.
I should have died from it then. But
if I had, Jalka would have been free
to leave the island. Free to attack the
people of Avantia. I am a Mistress of
the Beasts, and I could not let that
happen. So instead I've lived with it,
every day since then."

Tom nodded. There was a lump in

his throat, but he understood.

"That's why you joined yourself to the Beast," he said. "You stopped Jalka. But in return, you've been in torment for sixty years."

"Until you came to rescue me, Tom," said Kara. Her face was white, but she was still smiling. "Now my Quest is over at last. I die happy, knowing that the kingdom is safe. Hail Tom, Master of the Beasts."

Tom gripped her hand in his, and did his best to return the smile. "Hail Kara," he said, "Mistress of the Beasts..."

"It is time," Kara said, wincing. "Time for me to take my place beneath the palace, in the Gallery of Tombs." She turned to Aduro. "You look familiar, in a strange way. I see you wear a wizard's robes. Perhaps you knew my brother, Mivan?"

Aduro eyes were moist as he came forward and rested a gnarled hand on Kara's shoulder. "I was just a boy when I met you, Kara. My name is Aduro, and I was apprentice to your brother."

Kara managed a smile. "So much time has passed..."

"Farewell, Kara," said Aduro, his tears rolling down his cheeks. "Tell my master Mivan that Aduro – I mean to say, young Addie – sends his warmest greetings."

Kara nodded. Then she let out one last breath and closed her eyes. Gradually, her body began to fade away...

She's going to the Gallery of Tombs, thought Tom. *The resting place for every Master and Mistress of Beasts. Along with*

Tanner, and Taladon, and so many other brave men and women. And still, she is among the bravest.

"Goodbye, Kara," he said.

Tom held the silver axe flat on his palms as he laid it on the sarcophagus. It was dark and silent in the cavernous Gallery of Tombs, beneath King Hugo's palace in the City, and the scrape of metal on marble echoed as Tom stepped back next to Elenna, his head bowed.

The tomb was of jet-black stone, with a single word newly carved on its surface.

Kara.

Next to it was a matching black stone sarcophagus that had stood in the Gallery for many years. It bore

the name *Mivan*.

Wizard and warrior. Brother and sister. Together again.

Tom sighed. An Avantian mystery had been solved, and a great Mistress of the Beasts had found her resting place at long last.

Sepron had carried them home, and now Aduro was safely back in his study where he belonged, making some adjustments to Kara's chapter in the *Chronicles*, with the help of Daltec. The people of Krikos were free of their Armoured Queen at last, and King Hugo had sent envoys and craftsmen to help them rebuild their ruined homes.

The Quest was over. But all the same, Tom's heart was heavy. Who knew what he could have learned from Kara? What memories had died with her?

Elenna cleared her throat, sending echoes around the Gallery.

"Do you ever think about it?" she said quietly.

"About what?"

Elenna gestured at the countless

tombs, stretching out into the shadows on either side. "One day you'll be here, Tom, alongside all the other great heroes of Avantia."

Tom nodded. "I've thought about it. More and more since Taladon's final battle." He turned and led the way to the steps, climbing towards the light. "But I try not to. I have a feeling that many more Quests lie ahead of me.

There is so much to be done before I end my days here, in the Gallery of Tombs."

"There certainly is," said Elenna. Tom noticed she was grinning. "For one thing, I need to finish beating you at that game of *Peril!*"

Tom grinned back at her. After all they'd been through, it warmed his heart to see his friend so cheerful, so ready for the next adventure.

Whatever lies ahead, and wherever I go, she'll go with me.

"Come on then," he said. "But let's make it best of three!"

Have you read all the books in the
latest Beast Quest series,
THE CURSED DRAGON?
Out now!

FREE COLLECTOR CARDS INSIDE!

Beast Quest®
THE CURSED DRAGON

Series 14: THE CURSED DRAGON
COLLECT THEM ALL!

Tom must face four terrifying Beasts as he searches for the ingredients for a potion to rescue the Cursed Dragon.

978 1 40832 920 7

978 1 40832 921 4

978 1 40832 922 1

978 1 40832 923 8

Win an exclusive
Beast Quest T-shirt and goody bag!

In every Beast Quest book the Beast Quest logo is
hidden in one of the pictures. Find the logo in this book
and make a note of which page it appears on.
Write the page number on a postcard and
send it in to us.
Each month we will draw one winner to receive
a Beast Quest T-shirt and goody bag.

THE BEAST QUEST COMPETITION:
JAKARA THE GHOST WARRIOR
Orchard Books
338 Euston Road, London NW1 3BH
Australian readers should email:
childrens.books@hachette.com.au

New Zealand readers should write to:
Beast Quest Competition
PO Box 3255, Shortland St, Auckland 1140, NZ.
or email: childrensbooks@hachette.co.nz

Only one entry per child.
Closing date: 30 May 2015

You can also enter this competition
via the Beast Quest website: www.beastquest.co.uk

Fight the Beasts,
Fear the Magic

Do you want to know more
about BEAST QUEST?
Then join our Quest Club!

Visit
www.beastquest.co.uk/club
and sign up today!

Beast Quest ®

⟫ Series 1 ⟪
COLLECT THEM ALL!

Have you read all the books in Series 1 of
BEAST QUEST? Read on to find out where
it all began in this sneak peek from book 1,
FERNO THE FIRE DRAGON...

FERNO
THE FIRE DRAGON

978 1 84616 483 5

SEPRON
THE SEA SERPENT

978 1 84616 482 8

ARCTA
THE MOUNTAIN GIANT

978 1 84616 484 2

TAGUS
THE HORSE-MAN

978 1 84616 486 6

NANOOK
THE SNOW MONSTER

978 1 84616 485 9

EPOS
THE FLAME BIRD

978 1 84616 487 3

CHAPTER ONE

THE MYSTERIOUS FIRE

Tom stared hard at his enemy. "Surrender, villain!" he cried. "Surrender, or taste my blade!"

He gave the sack of hay a firm blow with the poker. "That's you taken care of," he announced. "One day I'll be the finest swordsman in all of Avantia. Even better than my father, Taladon the Swift!"

Tom felt the ache in his heart that always came when he thought about his father. The uncle and aunt who had brought Tom up since he was a baby never spoke about him or why he had left Tom to their care after Tom's mother had died.

He shoved the poker back into its pack. "One day I'll know the truth," he swore.

As Tom walked back to the village, a sharp smell caught at the back of his throat.

"Smoke!" he thought.

He stopped and looked around. Through the trees to his left, he could hear a faint crackling as a wave of warm air hit him.

Fire!

Tom pushed his way through the trees and burst into a field. The golden wheat had been burned to black stubble and a veil of smoke hung in the air. Tom stared in horror. How had this happened?

He looked up and blinked. For a second he thought he saw a dark shape moving towards the hills in the distance. But then the sky was empty again.

An angry voice called out. "Who's there?"

Through the smoke, Tom saw a figure stamping around the edge of the field.

"Did you come through the woods?" the man demanded. "Did you see who did this?"

Tom shook his head. "I didn't see a soul!"

"There's evil at work here," said the farmer, his eyes flashing. "Go and tell your uncle what's happened. Our village of Errinel is cursed – and maybe all of us with it!"

Read FERNO THE FIRE DRAGON to find out what happens next...

IF YOU LIKE BEAST QUEST, YOU'LL LOVE ADAM BLADE'S NEW SERIES

Deep in the water lurks a new breed of Beast!

978 1 40831 848 5   978 1 40831 849 2   978 1 40831 850 8   978 1 40831 851 5

978 1 40832 411 0   978 1 40832 412 7   978 1 40832 413 4   978 1 40832 414 1

978 1 40832 853 8   978 1 40832 855 2   978 1 40832 857 6   978 1 40832 859 0

31901060040930

COLLECT THEM ALL!

www.seaquestbooks.co.uk